THE TICKLE STORIES

by Jean Van Leeuwen   pictures by Mary Whyte

DIAL BOOKS FOR YOUNG READERS ⚘ NEW YORK

Published by Dial Books for Young Readers
A member of Penguin Putnam Inc.
375 Hudson Street
New York, New York 10014

Designed by Julie Rauer
Printed in Hong Kong
First Edition
1 3 5 7 9 10 8 6 4 2

Library of Congress Cataloging in Publication Data
Van Leeuwen, Jean.
The tickle stories/by Jean Van Leeuwen; pictures by Mary Whyte.—1st ed.
p. cm.
Summary: Grandpop's fanciful tales of ticklish worms, cows, and toes
help three rambunctious children get ready for bed.
ISBN 0-8037-2048-3 (trade).—ISBN 0-8037-2049-1 (lib. bdg.)
[1. Bedtime—Fiction. 2. Storytelling—Fiction.
3. Grandfathers—Fiction.] I. Whyte, Mary, ill. II. Title.
PZ7.V3273Tf 1998 [E]—dc21 97-22107 CIP AC

The full-color artwork was prepared using watercolor washes. It was
then scanner-separated and reproduced as red, blue, yellow, and black halftones.

For David and Elizabeth, who always needed stories,
songs, tickles, and five kinds of kisses

J.V.L.

To Bob and Dodie, with love and laughter

M.W.

It was bedtime. But where were the children?

Jumping on beds and rolling around on the floor, that's where. Beating on drums and building block towers and dressing up in hats, that's where.

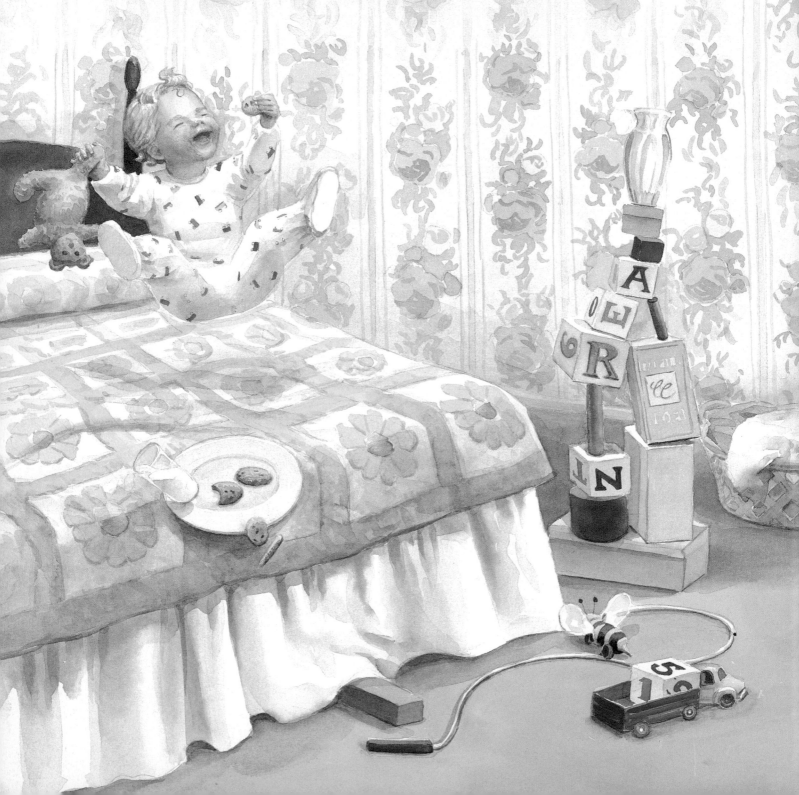

"Children!" called Grandpop. "Time for bed."

"We don't want to go to bed," said Maggie.

"It's too early," said Morgan.

"Too hot," said Baby Max.

"Too bad," said Grandpop. "Under the covers now, lickety-split."

Maggie and Morgan and Baby Max jumped into bed.

"Good night, my little chickadees," said Grandpop.

"We can't go to sleep," said Maggie. "First we need hugs. And kisses. Mama always gives us five different kinds: smackers, whispers, butterflies, Eskimo, and sloppy wet."

"And she sings us a song," said Morgan.

"And Papa tickles our toes," said Baby Max.

"This bedtime thing is a lot of work," grumbled Grandpop.

But he did the hugs and kisses, five different kinds, and the song and the toe tickles. Then he turned off the light. "Good night, my little chickpeas."

"You can't go yet," said Maggie. "You forgot the story."

Grandpop sighed and lay down with his eyes closed so he looked like he was asleep. He even gave a couple of little snores. But then his mouth opened and he began to tell a story.

"Once upon a time when I was young—oh, about a hundred years ago—I lived on a farm. We had cows on our farm, and horses and pigs and chickens. But the best thing we had every summer was my thirty-seven cousins."

"Thirty-seven?" said Maggie.

"Well, seventeen."

"Really?" said Morgan.

"Okay, seven. But they seemed like more."

"What were their names?" asked Baby Max.

"Who's telling this story anyway?" said Grandpop.

"Ssshhh," said Maggie.

And they all snuggled down, cozy as kittens, and listened.

"That summer was the hottest one ever. It was so hot that the horses were fanning each other with their tails. Sunflowers lay down in the shade. And when we collected the eggs from the chickens, they were already cooked. Hard-boiled mostly, but a few were sunny-side up.

"My cousins Big George and Little Georgie and Polly and Priscilla and Archie and Tom and Lucy and my big brother Jake and my little brother Ike and I liked to have fun. But even we didn't feel like riding the big old farm horses or sliding down the hayloft or picking blackberries. All we wanted to do was lie on our backs in the cool water of the swimming hole.

"Well, we did so much swimming we were getting wrinkled like prunes. So one day we decided to go fishing instead. We dug up some worms and sat in the shade, waiting for the fish to bite. We sat there and we sat there, but nothing happened. It was so quiet I could hear Big George growing. One by one I saw my cousins drop off to sleep.

"Now, one thing I always hated was too much quiet. Propping up my pole, I slipped into the water. Down I went, until I could look up. Just as I suspected, it wasn't only my cousins who were snoozing. Everything was: fish, frogs, water bugs, worms on their hooks. All of a sudden I had an idea.

"I swam over to a worm and gave it a tickle. It woke up with a wiggle. On I went: tickle-wiggle, tickle-wiggle. I tickled a frog. It woke up and saw a water bug. A fish woke up and saw a worm. Gulp!

"Suddenly frogs were jumping and lines were pulling and cousins were waking up. I jumped out just in time to grab my pole. Everyone was reeling in fish like crazy. Then Little Georgie fell in and Big George jumped in after him, creating a tidal wave, and there was a tremendous uproar.

"When things finally calmed down, we had caught twelve fish, Aunt Sally's straw hat, and an old shoe. Polly said her fish was the biggest, ha ha! She was my worst cousin. I said mine was, so we went to show them to the grown-ups.

"'Amazing,' said Aunt Sally.

"'What did you do to those worms?' asked Uncle Wilbur.

"And the strange thing was no one believed it when I told them," said Grandpop.

"What did you tell them?" asked Maggie.

"I tickled their tummies," said Grandpop. "Like this."

And he tickled their tummies till Maggie laughed so hard tears rolled down her cheeks and Baby Max nearly fell off the bed and Morgan said, "More!"

"More tummy tickles?" said Grandpop.

"More stories," said Morgan.

"Hmmmm," said Grandpop. He stretched out flat and was quiet awhile. Then he said, "I could tell you about the cows."

"Yes!" said Morgan.

"Cows are my best animal," said Baby Max.

"Mine too," said Grandpop. "Some folks say they can't tell one cow from another, but we had three dozen and we knew every one by name. So when this hot spell came along, we felt real sorry for the cows.

"**W**ell, one day we were milking Mabel and Bertha and Harriet and Gertie—she was my favorite—and oh my, those cows were miserable. Didn't have the energy to flick their tails at a fly, but then the flies didn't have the energy to bite anyway. My cousin Archie was sucking on a chunk of ice and he gave Gertie some, and that seemed to perk her up a little. Then I reached over and gave her a little tummy tickle, just to cheer her up.

"Nothing happened. I tried tickling her neck and her knees and under her chin. Gertie just looked at me. Cows must not be ticklish, I figured. Then I tickled her ear.

"Well, that cow just went crazy. She started giggling and jiggling and snickering and snorting. I tickled her other ear. She chuckled and chortled and danced a little jig.

"'Gertie!' said my papa, who was milking her. Then he stared down at the milk pail. 'Well, would you look at that!'

"We couldn't believe our eyes. Instead of a pail of milk, that cow had given a pail of ice cream.

"No one could figure it out. Until Archie remembered the ice. And I remembered the tickles. Archie ran for more ice and we fed it to the other cows and tickled them up, and pretty soon we had pails and pails of ice cream. Polly had to show how smart she was by feeding Bertha the berries she'd picked, so hers came out strawberry. And we had the coolest, most delicious ice cream party ever. We ate so much we couldn't move, but just lay around in the hay with the barn kittens the rest of the day.

"So now you know what to do," said Grandpop, "if you run across a grumpy cow."

"What?" said Morgan.

"Why, tickle her ears, of course."

And he tickled their ears till Morgan laughed so hard his tummy hurt and Baby Max hid under the covers and Maggie cried, "Stop!"

"Okeydokey," said Grandpop. "Well, good night, my little bumblebees."

"Not the stories," said Maggie.

"One more," said Baby Max. "Please?"

"One more," said Grandpop. "This one is a bedtime story.

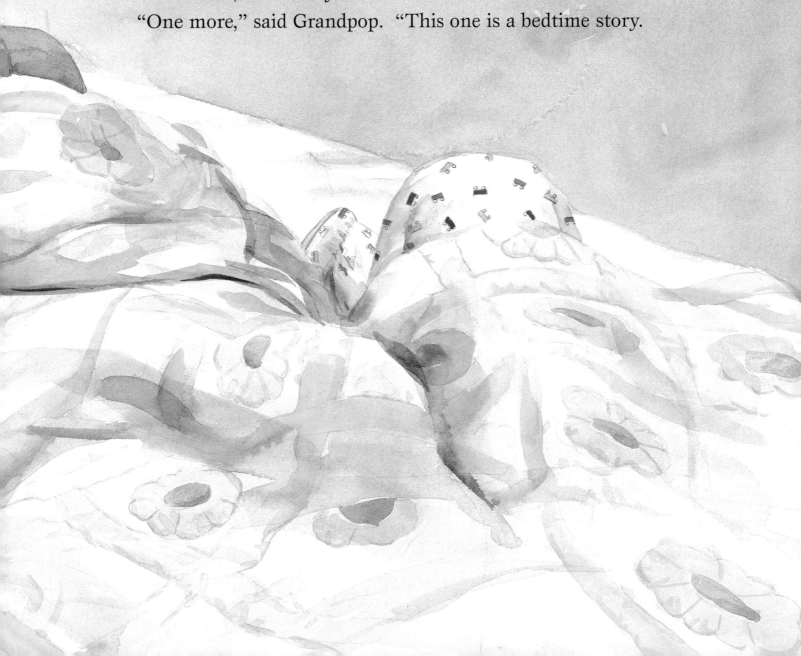

"**I guess I mentioned** how hot it was that summer. It never seemed to cool off, not even at night. It was so hot that the owl outside my window said, 'Whew' instead of 'Who.' Because there were so many cousins, we had to share beds, and half the time we ended up kicking off our blankets and kicking each other onto the floor.

"One night I'd gotten kicked out of bed so many times by Big George that I decided not to get back in. Instead I took my pillow and went downstairs to the porch. I lay in a hammock, looking up at the stars and feeling almost peaceful.

"Well, that lasted about a minute. Next thing I knew, my brother Jake was in the other hammock. Polly settled in on the porch swing. And Big George was telling me to move over and make room for him. Cousins were draped all over the porch.

"'We're having a camp out!' said Little Georgie.

"I tried to go to sleep. But so many cousins so close made it seem hotter than ever. And Big George's big feet were right in my face. So I just reached over and tickled his toes.

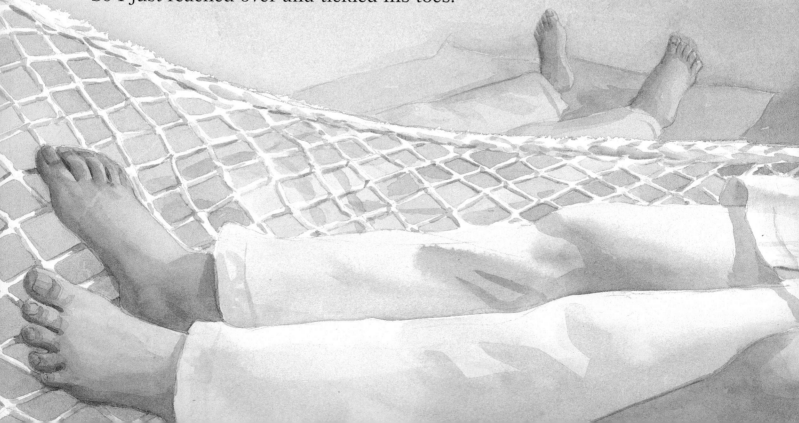

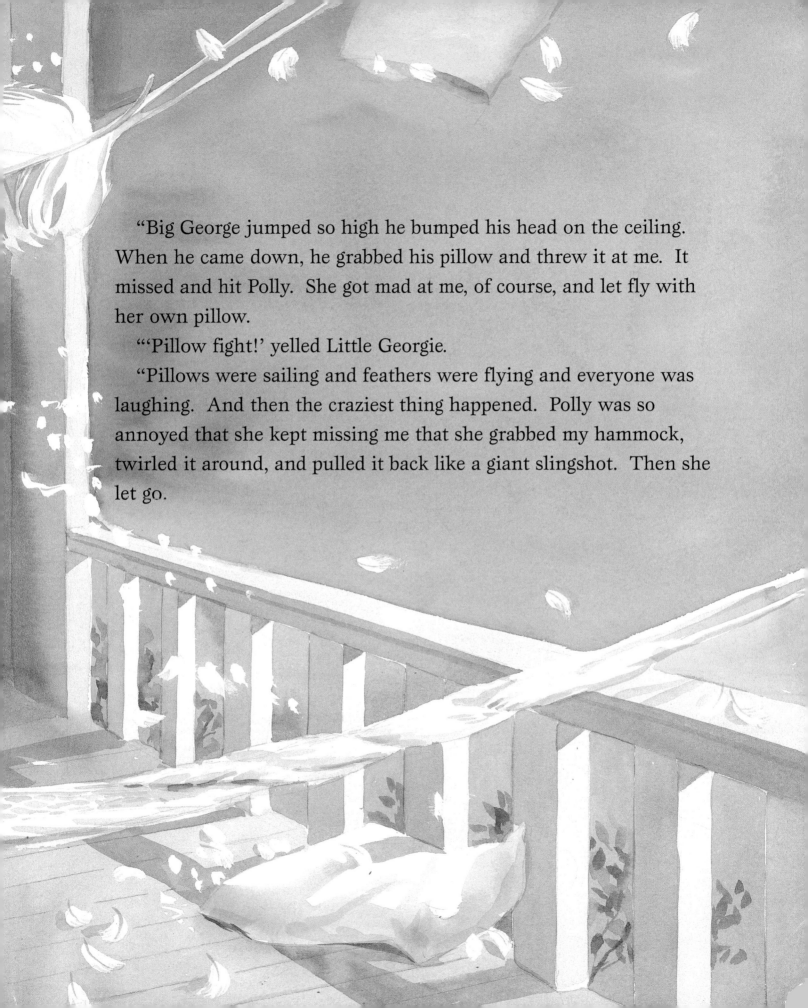

"Big George jumped so high he bumped his head on the ceiling. When he came down, he grabbed his pillow and threw it at me. It missed and hit Polly. She got mad at me, of course, and let fly with her own pillow.

"'Pillow fight!' yelled Little Georgie.

"Pillows were sailing and feathers were flying and everyone was laughing. And then the craziest thing happened. Polly was so annoyed that she kept missing me that she grabbed my hammock, twirled it around, and pulled it back like a giant slingshot. Then she let go.

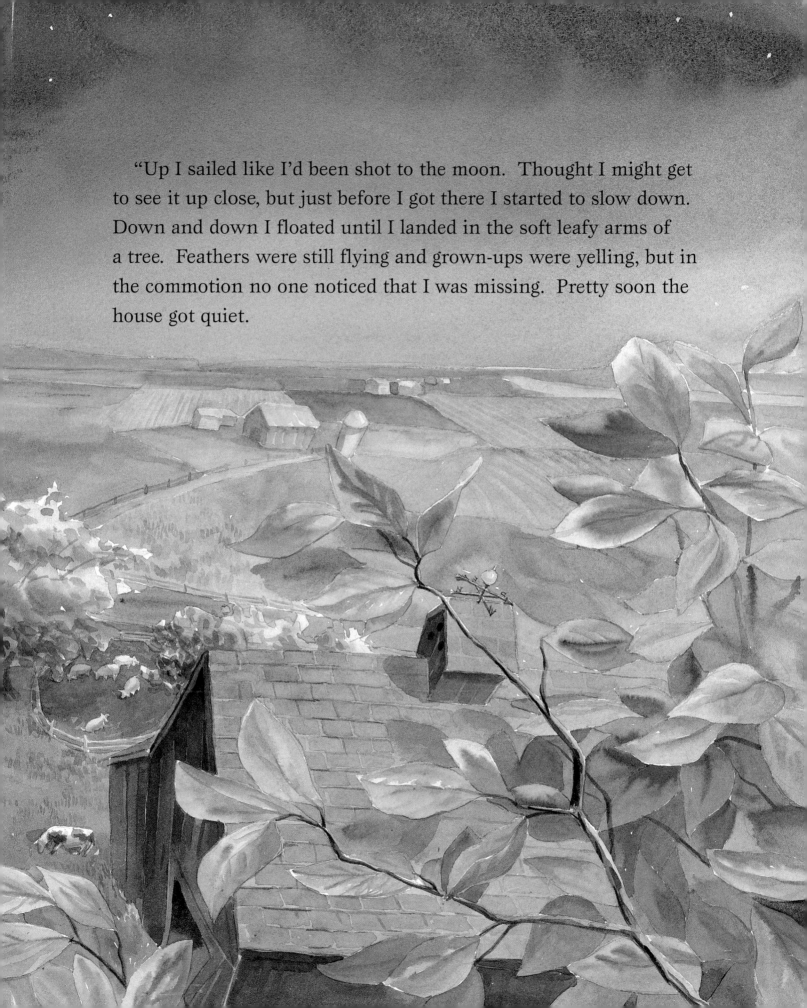

"Up I sailed like I'd been shot to the moon. Thought I might get to see it up close, but just before I got there I started to slow down. Down and down I floated until I landed in the soft leafy arms of a tree. Feathers were still flying and grown-ups were yelling, but in the commotion no one noticed that I was missing. Pretty soon the house got quiet.

"So I lay in my comfy bed in the tree, looking up at a million stars, and there was a tiny breeze and finally, *finally* I felt cool. And I fell asleep. Just like you are going to do now."

"But what about the toe tickles?" Baby Max asked sleepily.

"Here they come," said Grandpop.

And he tickled their toes, light as a feather, till they all three smiled and snuggled down, hugging their pillows.

"Good night, my little fricassees," said Grandpop.

"Good night," said Maggie and Morgan and Baby Max.

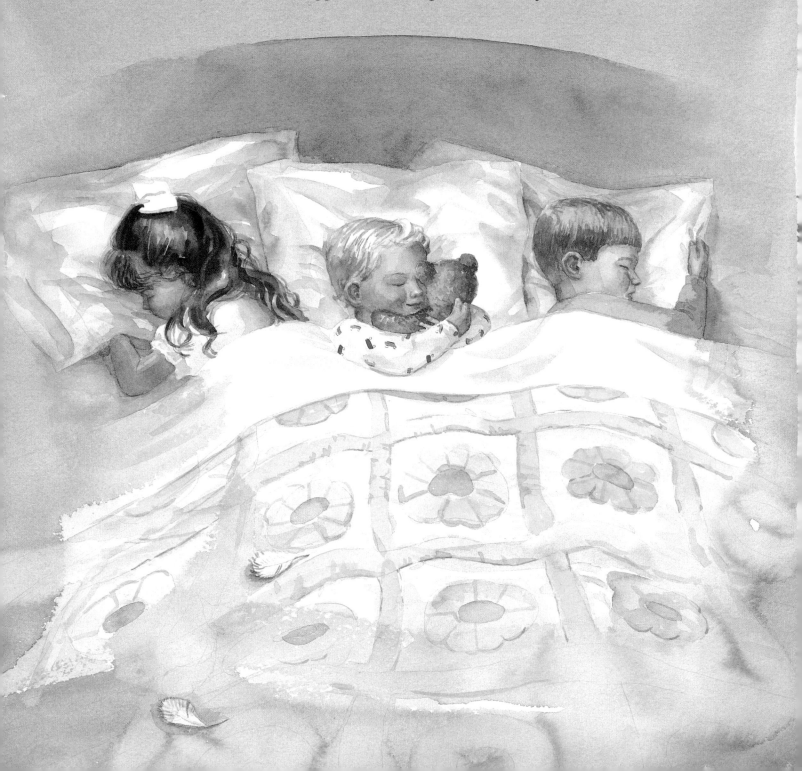